This book belongs to

....

ISBN 978-1-64638-878-3

www.cottagedoorpress.com

Cottage Door Press® and the Cottage Door Press® logo are
registered trademarks of Cottage Door Press, LLC.

I Spy with My Little Eye

EASTER HOP & FIND

Written by Rubie Crowe
Illustrated by Melanie Demmer

cottage door press

Easter Bunny, you've overslept!
Please wake up! Rise and shine!
It's very late already and we're
running so behind.

Can you find the
other bunny slipper?

The Easter Bunny has a great, big family.
Can you spot a picture of his mom?
She's reading under a tree.

I spy with my little eye a basket, plain and small. But this magic little basket holds the Easter Bunny's treats for one and all!

He sometimes likes a late-night treat. Can you count 6 carrots and 2 beets?

Oh, we'll be fine, my little friend. Please, calm down. Don't dismay.

I promise that today will be the perfect Easter Day!

See, there's nothing to fret about.
Everything is looking good!
The factory is running just
exactly as it should.

Can you find
4 more polka-dot
eggs like this one?

Some of these jelly beans
aren't bean-shaped at all!
Can you spot ones that look
like a heart, star, and ball?

We're all packed up and ready, time to shake a bunny tail.

The egg-mobile can navigate anyplace! But can you spot a road map, just in case?

Can you find 5 eggs that didn't make it into the Easter Bunny's basket?

Did you know the Easter Bunny has a pit crew?
Can you spot 3 mechanics and 3 wrenches, too?

Can you find the bunny with a purple hat?

Everybody came to cheer
the Easter Bunny on his way.
Do you see someone who
might be more at home
helping load Santa's sleigh?

Let's get this egg-mobile headed
down the bunny trail!

All right, this stop went very well.
I'm feeling calmer now.

A baby horse is called a foal.
Can you spot one who's
as black as coal?

It's his job to crow rise and shine!
Is there a rooster you can find?

Little piglets love Easter, too.
I spy 3 around, can you?

Can you count
8 Easter eggs hidden
at the farm?

I love to visit all the farms and
meet the baby cows.

Another successful stop out in the quiet woods.

Can you spot 10 jelly beans scattered around the forest?

Can you spot the bird taking a rest to sit on the eggs in her nest?

Normally squirrels gather nuts and seeds, but this one is storing Easter treats. Can you find him?

Can you find a sweet bear cub on the hunt for Easter grub?

I spy a deer wearing flowers and a bow. Where did she get those? Nobody knows! Do you see her, too?

We're keeping to our schedule and our time is looking good!

It's tricky hiding Easter treats when people live on boats.

I spy an alligator who wants to save her treat for later. Can you find her, too?

Can you find a hopping frog? Can you spot 2 turtles on a log?

Can you find 4 eggs floating in tubes?

Can you spot a playful otter sliding down into the water?

Luckily, we've come prepared— with lots of rafts and floats!

So, this year let's stick around
and give ourselves a treat.

Care for a little pick-me-up?
Can you find 5 fancy teacups?

I spy someone who raced
too fast and dropped
their egg into the grass.
Can you spot him?

Find the dog dressed like a chick.
He doesn't like it, not one bit.

I spy 3 Easter baskets.
Do you see them, too?
1 is pink and 2 are blue.

And see how people celebrate
Easter on Main Street!

Enjoy a slice of carrot cake
and smell the daffodils...

They have fur that's
warm and fluffy.
Spot 2 stripy bunny stuffies.

This necktie looks like a carrot.
Can you find it?
Would you wear it?

Look at all these tasty bakes!
Can you count 9 pink cupcakes?

I spy 3 wind-up chicks that hop.
Can you find them around the shop?

And hunt for painted Easter eggs across the grassy hills.

Most kids have baskets to hold their loot, but can you spot someone using a cowboy boot?

Can you find 2 kids wearing bunny tails?

I'm not pulling your leg. Can you spot some socks with Easter eggs?

The gold egg holds a special prize. Can you spot it? What's inside?

Just my luck! I was looking for candy, but I found a duck. Can you find me?

Can you find the Easter egg that matches this one?

Or stop to watch the parade as it marches down the way.

There are so many silly hats,
but can you spot:
1 filled with 2 fluffy chicks
and 1 made from a flower pot?

Can you find a little tyke riding on a bright pink trike?

Can you count 13 people wearing pink bunny ears?

Can you spot a friend from the farm who came to watch the parade?

There are lots of birds up in the sky.
Most are flying, but not this guy.
Can you find him?

I see a yummy
chocolate bunny.
Can you go back
and find one in
every scene?

I spy a balloon shaped
like an Easter egg.
Can you find it, too?

Can you spot
5 high-flying kites?

This hot-ballooner came
prepared—with a large pizza
to share! Can you find him?

You were right!
This really was the perfect Easter Day!